My name is

Julianna

& I have the
Power to Choose!

Dear Reader,

There are eight different stories in this book! When you reach an ending, you can start over and make different choices to see how my day changes. The guide below will help you understand the symbols.

Turn to the next page.

Turn to the page that your choice says to go to, and continue reading from there.

This shows you which page you came from, so ONLY use it if you want to go back and change your last choice.

You've reached one of the eight different endings! To reach another ending, start at the beginning and make different choices. Try to reach all eight!

Ganit & Adir Levy

What Should Darla Do?

Illustrated by Doro Kaiser

Hi! I'm Darla, and I'm an astronaut-in-training. That means I'm obsessed with space because it's the coolest thing ever!

Did you know that in space everything floats? So to get to Mars, I have to practice:

space flips,

space eating,

and flying a rocket ship.

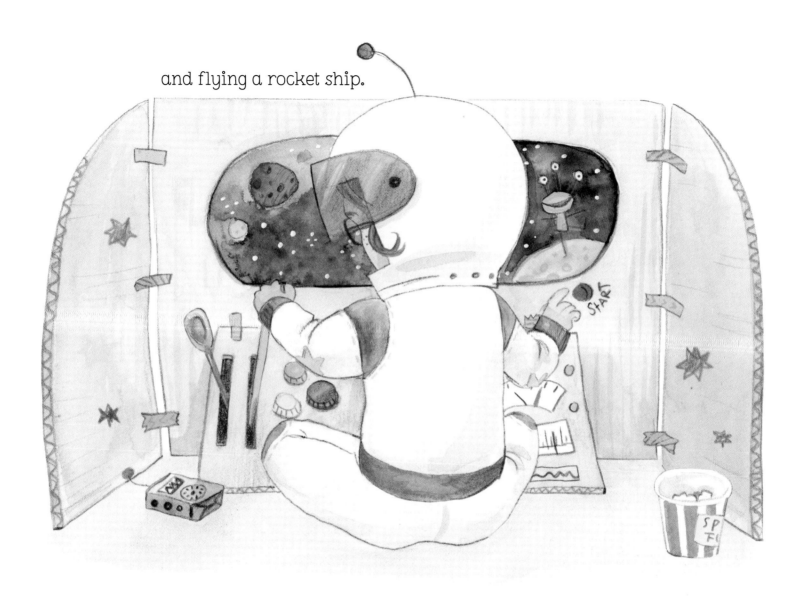

I also have to practice lots of other things that are really hard.
Luckily, I have a special superpower called the POWER TO CHOOSE.
With that power, I can change my day, and even my life,
with the choices I make!

Today, I'm getting ready for a special day because you'll be making choices for me!

When you get to an ending, you can start over and make different choices. Then, we'll see how the POWER TO CHOOSE changes my day.

I save the most important step for last: my cape, of course! My cousin Danny gave it to me for my birthday. Now, I'm finally ready. Let's go!

I blast to the breakfast table and see my brother.
"Good morning, Benjie!" I give him a big squishie hug.

Just before I sit down, my sister Hannah sits right next to him!

"Hey, I wanted to sit next to Benjie," I say.

"Too bad," Hannah replies. "I got here first."

What Should Darla Do?

Sit in a different chair? Go to page 14
Try to force Hannah off the chair? Go to page 40

I rush over and try to grab
the baking set out of her hands.
She pulls back as hard as she can.

We keep tugging till
the entire set falls and
breaks into pieces.

45

"You broke it!" I yell.

"Nu-uh, you did!" she says.

Now I'll never be able to use it again! I grab Astronautica and rush to my room to cry.

After lunch, I remember that the rocket ship I built yesterday needs a final touch of paint.

Hmmmm. Hannah has some glitter paint that I know will make the rocket look extra shimmery!

She didn't ask to borrow my baking set, so I'm not so sure I should ask to borrow her glitter paint.

What Should Darla Do?

Take Hannah's glitter paint without asking? Go to page 18

Ask to borrow Hannah's glitter paint? Go to page 72

"OK, I guess it's not such a big deal," I say.

I sit on the other side of the table. Benjie eats his yogurt and fruit with his hands. Yuck! Hannah and I laugh at the mess he makes!

9

Mommy asks us to clear the table and take out the trash.

"I got the dishes," Hannah says.

"I got the food," I say.

"I got the yogurt monster!" Mommy laughs.

When the table is clear, I take out the trash.

Just as I walk out, Zoe is riding by on a scooter.

"Hey, Darla! Want to come ride with me?" she asks.

"Yeah!" I say. "Let me ask my mom."

Mommy says yes, so I grab my
helmet and run outside.

We take turns doing bunny hops.
We're getting good!

"Race you to the corner," Zoe says.

"You're on!" I say.

We blast down the street, and
the race is super close. But then
I see an ultra rare Mitsy Glitsy
unicorn lying on the grass in
front of Sofia's house.

"Look what I found!" I say.

"Awww, you're so lucky," Zoe says. "I've wanted a Mitsy Glitsy for sooooo long! Let's take it back to your house and play with it!"

What Should Darla Do?

Take the unicorn home? Go to page 50
Check to see if it belongs to Sofia? Go to page 28

I grab the glitter paint and blast to my room.

Just as I begin painting my rocket, Hannah comes in.

"Hey! That's my glitter paint!" she says.

"Yeah, so? You weren't using it."

Hannah gets really mad. She grabs the
paint bottle out of my hand and pushes
my rocket ship off the table.

It crashes to the floor, and the wing breaks off. Hannah
rushes out of the room.

"Noooooo!" I yell. Now my rocket will never be able to get to Mars.

Today was the absolute worst day ever! Hannah was so mean to
me, I didn't get to sit next to Benjie, my baking set broke, and now
my rocket broke too! I wonder what I could have done to make
this day better.

End
#2

"Hey, what's so funny?" I ask.

"I was spraying Zoe's hair with water," Hannah says, "but then the top of the spray bottle fell off, and all of the water spilled on her lap."

"So we came outside to dry off in the sun," Zoe adds. "And now we're laughing because it looks like I peed in my pants."

"It really does!" I say.

33

While we laugh, a great idea pops into my head!

"Do you guys want to get really soaked?" I ask. "Let's ask if
we can go to the pool at the park!"

We blast off to ask my mom.

"You've all behaved so well today. You deserve it!" she says.

"Yay!!!" we all cheer.

Hannah and I zoom to change into our bathing suits!
Zoe runs next door to ask her mom and changes into hers.

We have the best time swimming and splashing around at the pool!

Then, Zoe and I look up at the diving board. Our neighbor, Liam, is about to jump off!

We're both a bit scared to jump, but to become an astronaut I'm going to have to be super brave.

"Hey, Zoe," I say. "Watch me fly to the moon!"

I climb up the ladder one step at a time. Whoa! This is higher than I thought it was. Any higher, and I'd be in space!

"I'm Darla, and I choose to be brave!" I yell.

"BLAST OFF!!"

This was the best day ever! I'm so proud of how I used my POWER TO CHOOSE.

End #1

17

"I think we should see if this Mitsy Glitsy belongs to Sofia," I tell Zoe.

I knock on the door, and Sofia's dad opens it. I hear Sofia crying.

"Hi, Darla," Mr. Vargas says.

"Hi," I say. "Does this belong to Sofia? We found it right outside."

"Yes! We've been looking for it everywhere! Thank you so much!"

Sofia runs to the door. "Mitsy, you're back!" She grabs Mitsy Glitsy and gives her a big hug.

"Do you guys want to stay and play with my unicorns?" she asks us.

"Sure!" we say.

Mr. Vargas calls our moms and tells them how we returned Sofia's Mitsy Glitsy. Mommy is so proud of me.

When we're done playing, Zoe comes
over to my house.

I put Astronautica's helmet on, and we
lift off to practice our space walks.
Hannah braids her doll's hair.

"You're so good at braiding," Zoe says.

"Thanks," Hannah replies. "I can do one in your hair too."

They play with each others' hair for soooo long. Are they ignoring me?

I go to the bathroom, but when I come back, they're gone.
I search through the entire house, but I can't find them.

Then I hear them laughing in the backyard. I go outside and see them giggling and telling secrets. *What's so funny?* I wonder. Are they talking about me?

What Should Darla Do?

Ask them why they're laughing? Go to page 22
Get mad at Hannah for taking Zoe away? Go to page 56

YOU
ARE MY
BUCKET LIST

45

"Sure, you can play with it," I say.
"But please ask me next time
before you take one of my toys," I say.
"OK, that's fair," Hannah says.
"I was bored and wanted to bake.
Want to have a cupcake war?"
she asks.

"Hmmm. What about a Martian Cupcake War?" I suggest. "Who can make the grossest cupcakes of all?"

"And the loser has to eat one of the winner's cupcakes." Hannah says.

"Eew! You're on!"

After we bake and frost the cupcakes, I add a bit of salt,

some slimy **anchovies**,

a spicy **jalapeña**,

and a chunk of stinky **cheese**.

For the finishing touch,
I top them with a pinch of
rainbow sprinkles. I know
I'm going to win!

I look over at Hannah's cupcakes, and they're icky too. I see that she's adding anchovies like I did, but she's putting on even more.

Hey! Is she copying me?

What Should Darla Do?

Tell Hannah that she's cheating? Go to page 46
Tell Hannah that her cupcakes look awesome? Go to page 68

"No fair! You sat next to him yesterday!" I yell.
"It's my turn!"

"Nuh-uh!" she says. "You did!"

I force my way onto the chair, but she shoves me off. I fall on my tush.

"Hey!" I yell. I push her back and she falls.

We both try sitting on the chair and forcing each other off. I can barely get a bite of food into my mouth.

After another minute, Benjie announces,
"Mama, all done!"

Mommy comes to take him.

Now that Benjie is gone, I don't even care where I sit.
I move over to the next seat.

When we're done eating,
Mommy reminds us to clean up
and take out the trash.

We start putting things away, but we keep arguing over everything. "I took the trash out last time," I say. "Your turn."

"No way! You tried to steal my seat!" Hannah says. "You do it!"

We both push the trash bag, and it rips open. Stinky trash falls everywhere. YUCK!

Now there's even more to clean up.

When we're finally done cleaning, Hannah takes out the trash, but I'm still mad at her.

I go to my room to cool down for a while.

Later, I blast off with
Astronautica to the moon.

SWOOSH!

"This is good practice for
our mission to Mars,"
I say.

Then I see Hannah walking to the kitchen with my baking set.

"Hey, that's mine!" I yell.

"Yeah, but you're not even using it," she says.
"Can I please play with it?" Hannah asks.

What Should Darla Do?

Let her play with it, but tell her to ask before she takes it next time? Go to page 34
Take it away from her? Go to page 10

"Copycat!" I say. "The anchovies were my idea!"

"No way!" she says. "I added the anchovies first."

39

I reach to grab the anchovies off of her cupcake, but she moves, so I accidentally knock her cupcake to the floor.

"Aaaaaaaa!" Hannah yells. She reaches for one of my cupcakes and smushes it flat on the counter.

"Nooooo! You meanie!" I cry.

"You started it!" Hannah cries. Then, she wipes her gooey hand on my apron.

"Eeeeewww!" I shout.

I run to the bathroom to clean up. This day isn't going well at all.

Why did Hannah ruin my cupcake and get me all dirty? Maybe none of this
would have happened if I hadn't called her a copycat
and knocked her cupcake down.

I wonder how my day would have improved if
I'd used my Power to Choose wisely.

End
#3

"OK," I say as I look around.

We take the unicorn back to my house and zoom to my room.

17

I grab Astronautica and fly her through the air.

"Houston, this is Astronautica checking in from Mars,"
I say. "I've found an unidentified unicorn on
the polar ice cap."

"Hi, Astronautica," Zoe laughs. "I think you
should bring the unicorn back to
earth for examination."

"Great idea, Houston!" I say.

Zoe and I jump into my rocket ship and get ready to fly back to earth.

"T-minus 10 seconds and counting: 5...4...3...2...1! Ignition, and blast off!"

Just then, Hannah walks in.

"Awesome Mitsy Glitsy!" she says. "Where'd you get it?"

"It's Zoe's," I say quickly before Zoe can answer.

After Hannah leaves, we start feeling guilty about lying and playing with a toy that isn't really ours. This doesn't feel good. What if we get caught? What if the unicorn belongs to Sofia, and she's looking for it now? I grab Mitsy Glitsy and tuck her away in my drawer.

"Let's do something else," I say.

We play on my swing for a while, but neither of us enjoy it
because we're so worried. Then we hear the doorbell ring.
Uh-oh.

We nervously walk to the front door. Mommy answers.

"Hello," Sofia's dad says. "Have you or your girls seen Sofia's new unicorn? She was playing with it this morning and thinks she may have left it on our front lawn."

Mommy turns to look at me.

What Should Darla Do?

Tell them she took the unicorn? Go to page 64
Say she doesn't know where the unicorn is? Go to page 60

I run over to them.

"Hey!" I say. "Why did you guys leave me? I've been looking for you everywhere! And why are you telling secrets about me?"

"We're not even talking about you!" Hannah replies.

33

I'm not sure I believe her. "Well, Zoe is my friend, and she's supposed to be playing with me, not you."

"We just came outside to..."

Before Hannah can finish, I grab Zoe's arm and tell her to come play with me.

Zoe pulls her arm away and looks like she's going to cry. She starts talking, but I'm so upset I don't even hear what she's saying. "Are you coming to play with me or not?" I ask.

Zoe looks frustrated. "I want to go home."

After she leaves, I tell Hannah that it's all her fault.

"No, it's not. We were trying to tell you what happened, but you weren't listening!" she yells. She storms off, and I'm left there all alone.

This day was going so well until now. Why doesn't anyone want to play with me anymore?

I wonder if it's because of how I used my POWER TO CHOOSE.

End #4

"I haven't seen any unicorns today," I say.

"Hannah!" Mommy calls. "Have you seen a toy unicorn today?"

"You mean the Mitsy Glitsy Darla and Zoe were playing with?" Hannah says.

55

Mommy looks back at me. I don't like this feeling in my tummy.
I wish I would have stayed on Mars with Astronautica.
I feel my face turn really warm.

"Oh, ummm. Zoe and I found one, but we didn't
know it belonged to Sofia," I say.

"So we brought it here," Zoe adds.

I run to get it, and hand it straight to Sofia. Her face lights up.

"Mitsy Glitsy!" she exclaims.

Although Sofia is happy, Mommy doesn't look happy at all.

After Sofia and her dad leave, Mommy wants to have a talk.

"When we find something that doesn't belong to us, we should always try to find the owner. And when asked, we should always tell the truth."

I'm so embarrassed. I know I shouldn't have taken the unicorn and lied about it.

Maybe if I used my POWER TO CHOOSE wisely, I wouldn't have this icky feeling in my tummy.

I see Sofia crying, and I know I'd feel the same way if I lost Astronautica. I know it was wrong to take Milsy Glitsy.

"Zoe and I found her in front of your house," I tell Sofia's dad. "I'm so sorry we took her."

55

I run to grab Mitsy Glitsy and take her straight to Sofia.

"Mitsy Glitsy!" she yells. "I missed you so much!"

She hugs her tight.

"Thank you so much!" Sofia's dad says.

After they leave, Mommy takes me aside.

"Darla, I'm proud of you for admitting you took the unicorn," she says. "But you should never take something that doesn't belong to you."

"You're right, Mommy," I say. "I should have knocked on Sofia's door to ask if it was hers."

I blast to my room and write Sofia a letter.

Dear Sofia,
I'm so sorry I took your Mitsy Glitsy. I will never do that again. I hope you can forgiv me and that we can stil be freinds.

DARLA

End #6

"Wow!" I say. "Your cupcakes are awesomely gross!"

"Yours are pretty disgusting too!" she laughs.
"Those olive eyes were a great touch!"

39

We both agree it's a tie, so we need to find someone
else to eat them. We take our cupcakes to Mom.

"Hey, Mommy! We made you some super yummy
cupcakes!" I say. We both laugh.

She laughs, too. "Mmmmm. Looks delicious–
especially the anchovies."

Suddenly, Benjie grabs a handful of my anchovy cupcake and stuffs it in his mouth!

"Eeeewww!" we all say.

He seems to like it. "More!" he says.

Looks like he's part Martian after all!

We get the real toppings and decorate some human cupcakes. They turn out delicious!

Even though I didn't make a great choice at breakfast, I'm happy I used my POWER TO CHOOSE to turn my day around and make it better.

End #7

I think about how my day has been so far. Maybe Hannah hasn't been so nice to me because I've been mean to her. If I took her paint without asking, that would make her even more mad. I find her in the living room.

"Hey, Hannah," I say.

She looks at me and doesn't say a thing.

"I'm sorry for the mean things I did. Can we start over and be nice to each other from now on?"

13

She thinks. "OK, we can try that."

"Awesome! Do you want to help me paint my new rocket ship? Your glitter paint would be perfect for the top."

She smiles. "Sure."

We grab her glitter paint and blast to the back yard. After we finish painting, we get ready to shoot the rocket into space. I add the baking soda, and Hannah pours in the vinegar.

I'm so happy I used my Power to Choose to reset this day and make it so much better.

End #8

Hey! We're Ganit & Adir, and we love writing children's books! We're parents to four amazing kids and love teaching them about their POWER TO CHOOSE!

Hi, I'm Doro, and I'm an illustrator from Germany! I'm passionate about painting with watercolors and illustrating happy and colorful things for children.

For Eliyah, Liel, Orelle, and all girls around the world: Choose to create your future, rather than live it.

Dear Parents & Educators,

Children enjoy the book best, and
learn the most, when reading
through multiple versions of the
story. Because this may be your
child's first exposure to a story
in this format, you may need to
encourage them to make different
choices "just to see what happens."

Through repetition and discussion,
your child will be empowered with
their understanding that their
choices will shape their days, and
ultimately their lives, into what
they will be.

Ganit & Adir

What Should Darla Do? / by Ganit & Adir Levy.

Summary: Darla, an astronaut-in-training, learns the importance of making good choices.
Levy, Ganit & Adir, authors
Kaiser, Doro, illustrator
Klempner, Rebecca, editor
ISBN 9781733094658
Visit www.whatshoulddarlado.com
Printed in the United States of America
Reinforced binding
First Edition, November 2019
10 9 8 7 6 5 4 3 2 1